Crown of Blood

The story of Macbeth
by William Shakespeare

Retold by David Clayton

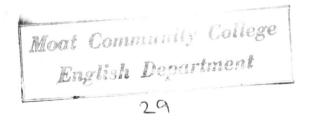

Illustrated by Mike Perkins
Series Editors: Steve Barlow and Steve Skidmore

Published by Ginn and Company
Halley Court, Jordan Hill, Oxford OX2 8EJ
A division of Reed Educational and Professional Publishing Ltd
Telephone number for ordering **Impact**: 01865 888084

OXFORD   MELBOURNE   AUCKLAND   JOHANNESBURG
BLANTYRE GABORONE   IBADAN   PORTSMOUTH (NH)
USA   CHICAGO

First published 1999

2003 2002 2001 2000

10 9 8 7 6 5 4

ISBN 0 435 21257 5

Illustrations
Mike Perkins

Cover artwork
Roger Harris / Folio

Designed by Shireen Nathoo Design

Printed and bound in Great Britain by Biddles

Contents

Characters

Lord Macbeth is Scotland's greatest soldier. He is Lord of Glamis and King Duncan's cousin.

Lord Macbeth

Lady Macbeth

Lady Macbeth is Lord Macbeth's wife.

Lord Banquo

Lord Banquo is Macbeth's best friend. He has a young son called Fleance.

King Duncan is King of Scotland. He is a good and fair King.

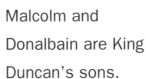

King Duncan

Malcolm and Donalbain

Malcolm and Donalbain are King Duncan's sons.

Lord Macduff

Lord Macduff is the Lord of Fife.

The story of Macbeth takes place in Scotland around 1000 years ago.

CHAPTER 1
One dark and evil day

The battle was over. The Scots had won
and the heads of the losers hung on poles.
The army marched through wind and rain.
They were going home.

Macbeth and Banquo were leaders of the army. They rode to King Duncan's castle to tell him about the battle.

"We won a great victory today!" said Banquo.

Macbeth pulled his cloak tightly around him. "Yes, it was a good day. But what a terrible night!"

The weather got worse as they rode across the moors. Strange eyes watched them. Three witches were waiting in the dark.

Now the battle is lost and won. Now it is time to meet Macbeth.

The witches suddenly blocked the soldiers' path. There was no way past.

One by one, the witches spoke to
Macbeth.

The witches' words shocked Macbeth.
The Lord of Cawdor was still alive and
Duncan was King.

"What's the matter?" asked Banquo.
"The witches say you will be King one day.
Why look so afraid?"

Macbeth did not reply. He was wondering
how the witches' words could ever come true.

11

Banquo turned to the witches. "Can you really see into the future?" he asked. "What will happen to me?"

The witches smiled.

The witches started to vanish into the mist. Macbeth charged forward.

"Wait! Don't go! Tell us more!"

But it was too late. The witches had gone.

CHAPTER 2
The King's message

"If only the witches had stayed longer,"
Macbeth said. "We could have found out
what they meant. They said your sons would
be Kings!"

"They said *you* would be King and Lord
of Cawdor!" Banquo replied.

As Banquo and Macbeth puzzled over the witches' words, two riders came thundering towards them.

As they spoke, Macbeth thought about what the witches had said.

I'm Lord of Cawdor, just as the witches said. Maybe I'll be King, too. But King Duncan would have to die first.

Macbeth turned to Banquo.

"Let's talk about the witches later, when we're on our own," he said.

Banquo nodded. "It's been a long day and a hard ride. Let's hurry home to greet the King. Then we can join the feast and drink all night!"

CHAPTER 3
A victory feast

Macbeth and Banquo rode swiftly to King
Duncan's castle. The victory feast had already
started. King Duncan praised Banquo and
Macbeth for winning the battle.

Then the King made a speech.

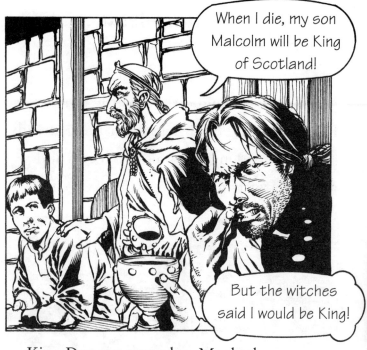

When I die, my son Malcolm will be King of Scotland!

But the witches said I would be King!

King Duncan turned to Macbeth.

"Macbeth, I will stay at your castle tomorrow night," he said.

Macbeth told the King he would be welcome. But his thoughts were turning to murder. He sent a message to his wife. Then he rode ahead to get the castle ready for King Duncan.

Chapter 4

The King must die!

At Macbeth's castle, Lady Macbeth opened the letter from her husband. She read about his victory and his meeting with the witches.

"The witches spoke the truth," she thought. "My husband must be King. But we'll have to kill Duncan!"

Then messengers arrived to say King Duncan was on his way. This was their chance! But would Macbeth be strong enough to commit murder? She prayed to the witches.

Witches! Make me hard and cruel. Make me strong enough to kill!

When Macbeth arrived, Lady Macbeth had made some plans.

"How long is King Duncan staying?" she asked.

"Just tonight," Macbeth said. "Tomorrow he will be on his way."

"No!" Lady Macbeth said. "Tonight King Duncan will die! You will be King."

Macbeth wanted more time to think. "Let us talk about it later," he said.

As the sky grew dark, King Duncan arrived at Macbeth's castle. Lady Macbeth hid her true feelings and welcomed him.

That night, Macbeth held a feast for the King. He thought about how trusting King Duncan was. Macbeth should be loyal to him rather than murder him! Macbeth went out of the hall for some air. Lady Macbeth followed him.

I've changed my mind about tonight. I'm Scotland's hero now. If I kill the King, I'll throw it all away!

Call yourself a man? You're a coward!

No one had dared call Macbeth a coward
before. He was a strong soldier. Would he
have to prove it by killing King Duncan?

"But what if it goes wrong?" Macbeth
asked.

It can't go wrong. We'll drug the guards and use *their* knives to kill the King. Then we'll cover the guards with blood. They will get the blame!

"Very well!" said Macbeth. "Let's return
to the feast. Afterwards, when Duncan
is asleep, we'll carry out our plan."

Chapter 5
The night of death

It was after midnight when the feast ended.
Macbeth went for a walk around his castle.
Banquo and his son Fleance were also awake.

"I dreamed about those witches last night," Banquo said to Macbeth. "Some of their words came true. But they said you would be King. Have you thought any more about it?"

This was the last thing Macbeth wanted to talk about. He did not want Banquo to suspect him of murdering King Duncan.

I haven't given the witches another thought. Don't let them spoil your sleep.

Banquo and his son went on their way. Macbeth called to a servant.

"Go and tell Lady Macbeth to ring the bell when my drink is ready."

Macbeth waited alone for the sound of the bell. It was the signal to kill. But as he waited, he saw a ghostly light. It moved towards him.

What is this … a dagger? It's dripping with blood! Is it real, or am I going mad?

The sound of the bell made Macbeth turn away.

"It's time to die, Duncan. Time for Heaven or for Hell!"

Macbeth went up to the King's room. His heart was beating fast. The guards were lying on the floor. Macbeth took their knives. He stood over the sleeping King. It was an easy kill. Too easy. Macbeth could not move.

"How can I stab my own King in his sleep?" he thought.

Then he remembered his wife's words.
He had to be King. He had to prove he was
a man!

In a daze, Macbeth went back downstairs to his wife.

Lady Macbeth took the knives upstairs. When she returned, Macbeth was looking at the blood on his hands. He was shaking.

"Pull yourself together!" his wife said. "My hands are red with blood like yours, but I'm not shaking!"

As Lady Macbeth spoke, the sound of knocking came from the castle gate.

Quick! Wash away the blood. No one must suspect us!

Trembling, Macbeth washed away Duncan's blood.

CHAPTER 6
Murder!

The porter staggered across the castle yard
to open the gate. He was half-drunk and
half-asleep, cold and grumpy. The knocking
started again.

"I'm coming!" he shouted.

He opened the gate. Lord Macduff and
Lord Lennox stood outside.

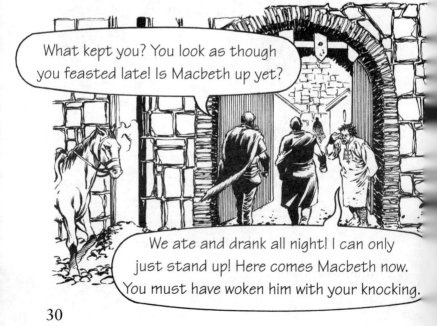

What kept you? You look as though
you feasted late! Is Macbeth up yet?

We ate and drank all night! I can only
just stand up! Here comes Macbeth now.
You must have woken him with your knocking.

Macbeth came to meet them. He was pretending to yawn.

"Welcome to my castle," he said.

"We've come for the King," Macduff said. "He asked me to be here at dawn. Is he up yet? We have a long journey to make."

Macbeth led the way to King Duncan's room. He stayed outside with Lennox while Macduff went in to wake the King.

Lennox told Macbeth that the night had been wild. There had been strange screams. People had terrible dreams. The earth itself had shaken.

But Macbeth's mind was not on what Lennox said. In seconds their lives would change forever.

The cry Macbeth had dreaded came from King Duncan's bedroom.

"MURDER!"

Macduff ran out, shouting.

Soon the whole castle was awake.

Everyone stood and stared in shock. Lady
Macbeth knew she had to take the attention
away from Macbeth. She crashed to the floor
in a faint. People rushed to help her.

King Duncan's sons, Malcolm and
Donalbain, took this chance to escape. Their
father had been murdered. It could be their
turn next! They left the castle quickly. They
would make plans, then take their revenge.

CHAPTER 7
A new King

Word of Duncan's murder quickly spread all over Scotland. Malcolm fled to England. Donalbain went to Ireland. Some people thought they were the murderers. Many people thought Macbeth had killed Duncan so he could be the King. But they couldn't prove it.

Nothing could stop Macbeth now. He was crowned King. It was a terrible day for Scotland. The witches' words had come true.

Macbeth held a feast in his castle that night. He asked Banquo to come as his special guest. But Macbeth had other plans for him.

Banquo and Fleance rode out of the castle. Macbeth called two men into his room.

The witches words came true for me. What if they come true for Banquo? Then his sons will be Kings instead of mine!

Macbeth turned to the men.

"Banquo and his son must die tonight," said Macbeth. "They are out riding. Kill them in the woods as they return."

Macbeth handed over a bag of money.

"It will be done!" said the murderers.

Lady Macbeth entered the room as the two men left. She saw Macbeth frown.

"Why aren't you happy?" she said. "The murder is done. You're the King!"

"Will I ever feel happy again?" Macbeth asked. "Sometimes I wish I was dead. And the murders aren't over yet!"

"What do you mean?" Lady Macbeth asked.

"You'll soon find out!" said Macbeth. "The witches' words to Banquo must never come true. His sons must never be Kings."

"People will suspect us if you're not careful!" said Lady Macbeth. "Pretend to be happy. Greet your guests with smiles at the feast tonight!"

CHAPTER 8
Danger in the dark

Out in the wood, the murderers waited for Banquo and his son. The sky was black with streaks of red.

They heard the sound of horses. Banquo and Fleance were riding back to the castle. The murderers' attack was sudden and violent.

Murder!! Run, Fleance!

The boy is getting away!

Fleance ran wildly through the wood. The
murderers could not catch him.

One of the murderers turned on the other.

"Macbeth isn't going to like this!" he said.
"We've killed Banquo. Why did you let
Fleance get away?"

CHAPTER 9
A strange guest

Back at the castle, guests were arriving for the feast. Macbeth greeted them with smiles. The servants filled their cups with wine. As Macbeth looked round, he noticed that Lord Macduff had stayed away.

"Macduff must suspect that I killed King Duncan," Macbeth thought. "This could mean trouble."

Then he noticed the murderers standing outside the hall. When nobody was looking, Macbeth slipped out.

"What are you doing here, with blood all over your face?" snapped Macbeth.

"It's Banquo's blood," said one of the murderers. "He doesn't need it any more. I cut his throat."

"What about the boy?" asked Macbeth.

He got away, my Lord.

So Fleance has escaped. He could still become King!

Macbeth sent the murderers away. Lady Macbeth came looking for him.

"We're waiting for you to start the feast!" she said. "Come and sit down."

Macbeth entered the hall. But as he went to sit down, a pale figure appeared in his chair. The ghost of Banquo had come to the feast.

The guests could not see the ghost. They wondered what was wrong with Macbeth.

Lady Macbeth tried to laugh it off. "Don't take any notice!" she said. "My husband is like this sometimes. Eat and drink! He'll soon feel better!"

As Banquo's ghost disappeared, Lady Macbeth turned to Macbeth. "You'll ruin everything!" she hissed. "Are you afraid of shadows?"

Banquo's ghost appeared again. Macbeth flung his cup at the terrible figure.

"Don't look at me like that!" he shouted. "I'm a brave soldier, but even I can't fight the dead!"

Lady Macbeth spoke quickly. "The King is getting worse," she said. "It's time to leave."

When the guests had gone, Lady Macbeth turned to Macbeth. "This is madness," she said. "You must get some rest."

But Macbeth's mind was racing.

I've killed so many people that there's no way back. Now Macduff suspects me. What shall I do about him? I must talk to the witches again. I need to find out what will happen.

CHAPTER 10
The witches' secrets

Macbeth rode back to the moor where he had first met the witches. Once again, they were waiting for him.

"Look!" said the witches. "Something evil is coming this way."

Macbeth got down from his horse.

Macbeth clenched his fists. "Tell me my future!"

"Watch, then," said the witches.

The witches' pot grew bright. A mist rose into the air and formed a shape.

The head faded. A second shape formed.
It was a baby, covered in blood.

The vision of the baby faded. A third vision rose into the air.

But Macbeth had one more question.

"I must know!" he said. "Will Banquo's sons ever be Kings?"

"Watch," said the witches. "But you will wish you had never asked!"

A final vision grew before Macbeth's
eyes.

Macbeth turned to the witches in disgust.
But they had gone.

Chapter 11
Revenge

That night, a messenger arrived with news.

"Macduff has gone to England. He's joined Malcolm's army. They are coming to fight you!"

"Where are Macduff's wife and children?" Macbeth asked.

"He left them at home in Fife," the messenger replied.

Macbeth smiled grimly.

"My men will pay them a visit," he said.

"Macduff will never see his family again!"

The news of the murder of Lady Macduff and her children spread quickly. Macduff's cousin went to England to tell Macduff and Malcolm the shocking news.

"Macduff," said Ross. "Your wife and children are dead. Macbeth has murdered them all, even your babies."

When Lady Macbeth heard about the murder of Macduff's family, she felt guilty and fell ill.

Then she started to walk and talk in her sleep. She wept, and rubbed her hands. Her servant asked a doctor to help.

CHAPTER 12
Time for battle

Macbeth stood on the battlements of his castle. He knew that Malcolm and Macduff's army was on its way.

Macbeth was not afraid. The witches had told him he could not be killed by a man born of a woman. They had also said that he was safe until Birnam Wood moved to his castle. That could never happen!

A soldier came with the news he was expecting.

"Malcolm and Macduff's army has arrived! They have camped the other side of Birnam Wood."

Macbeth sent the soldier away and stood alone.

It's time for battle, whether I win or die.
My life is empty. No happy old age for me!
I have no friends or honour.
Bring me my armour!

As Macbeth was strapped into his armour, the doctor arrived.

"I cannot do anything to help Lady Macbeth," the doctor said.

Macbeth could not talk about Lady Macbeth for long. The castle was ready for attack. Flags were flying. Drums were beating.

Suddenly, there was a terrible cry.

Macbeth ran into Lady Macbeth's room.

Why did you have to die now? Life has cheated me again! We struggle so hard but we end up with nothing.

Chapter 13
Tricked!

A messenger rushed into the room.

"My Lord! Birnam Wood is on the move. The trees are coming towards the castle!" he cried.

Macbeth was stunned. He ran to the window.

Malcolm and Macduff's army are using branches cut from the trees to hide behind. The witches have tricked me with their clever words!

Macbeth strode out of the castle. His sharp sword glittered in his hand. His army marched with him. Macbeth was a killer. He was not afraid.

Malcolm and Macduff's army threw aside their branches.

The killing began.

The witches said no man who was born of a woman could kill me. I'm safe!

"Macbeth!"

Macbeth twisted round as he heard
Macduff's angry voice.

Macbeth held his sword in front of him.
It was dripping with blood.

"Go away!" repeated Macbeth. "No man
who is born of a woman can kill me!"

Macduff's hard eyes stared at Macbeth.
He smiled grimly.

"Then your life is over, Macbeth! I was
cut from my mother's body before she could
give birth to me!"

Macbeth knew he was beaten.

"Another witches' promise that was a
clever trick!" he thought.

But he would fight to the end. He raised
his bloody sword.

Macduff charged towards him.

61

Macbeth and Macduff fought long and
hard. But Macduff found new strength when
he remembered his murdered family. He
struck the final blow.

The murderer was dead. Macduff cut off Macbeth's head and hung it on a pole. He gathered his men and marched to find Malcolm.

The battle was over.

Macbeth is dead! Scotland is safe again. Long live King Malcolm!

ABOUT THE AUTHOR

David Clayton is a writer and professional actor. Macbeth is his favourite play.

David lives in Cheshire with his family, his two sheep dogs, his cat and his computer.

IMPACT
RETELLING
SET D